Alissa
and the Castle Ghost

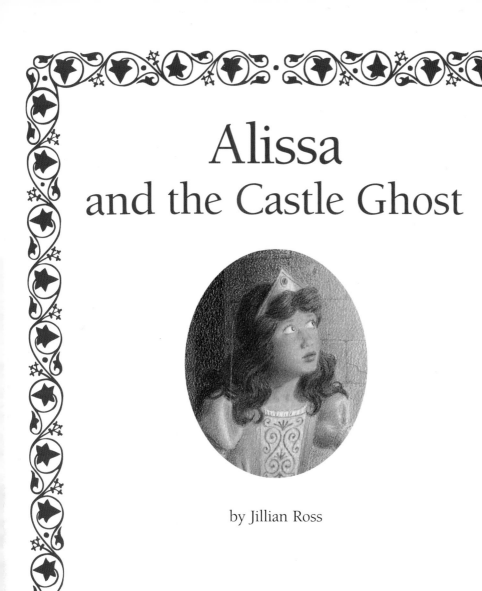

by Jillian Ross

Illustrations by Nick Backes

Spot Illustrations by
Katherine Salentine

Stardust
CLASSICS™

For more information, contact:
Just Pretend
1-800-286-7166

Stardust Classics is a registered trademark
of Just Pretend, Inc.

Design and Art Direction by Vernon Thornblad

First Edition
Printed in Hong Kong

04 03 02 01 00 99 98   10 9 8 7 6 5 4 3 2

Library of Congress Catalog Card Number 97-73129

ISBN 1-889514-07-1 (Hardcover)
ISBN 1-889514-08-X (Softcover)

Contents

CHAPTER ONE

The Mysterious Portrait

 just can't stand it!" Princess Alissa cried. She dusted her hands—which were covered with blue powder—on her long skirt.

Balin looked up from the book he was studying. "I'm sure you don't mean your rather messy gown," the wizard said.

Alissa looked down. For the first time, she noticed the blue spots on her dress. "Oh, bother," she said. "No, I didn't mean that. I meant my lessons with Sir Drear. I'm now expected to learn about every lord and lady who ever served Arcadia. Did I tell you that?"

"As a matter of fact, you did," replied the wizard. "Several times."

"I really can't stand it!" cried Alissa. "They're all old and dead and boring! And it just doesn't seem fair! Why must I study them and fine manners at the same time?"

"Ah yes," laughed Balin. "Your great-aunts Maude and Matilda still see a need for deportment lessons, don't they?"

"They'll never think my manners are good enough. At least not good enough for the future queen of Arcadia."

Alissa picked up the glass bottle she'd been filling. "Well, this is done," she said proudly. "A whole pint of powder for bringing summer rains." She gently placed it on a shelf crowded with other bottles.

1

As Alissa began cleaning up the mess she'd made, she looked around Balin's tower. The room was filled with wonders. Strange books of learning and magic. Rich tapestries covered with bright stars, suns, and moons. Odd doors that couldn't possibly lead anywhere, yet surely did. And a crystal ball that glowed with the colors of the rainbow.

Yes, the room was filled with wonders. But even wonders get dirty, thought Alissa. Especially when you've been mixing powders.

Alissa wiped off the long table at the center of the room. Then she returned to her complaint. "All these lessons take up too much time," she said. "I know my manners need a little more work. But I don't see why I have to study Arcadia's dusty old past too. I'd much rather be here with you, learning about magic."

"The past has much to tell you, Alissa," said Balin. "Don't forget that the secrets of magic are found in old books like this." He patted the thick book in his hands.

"Besides, I'm old—and quite dusty too," he added. Balin brushed the sleeve of his glittering robe. A small cloud rose into the air.

"You may be dusty," laughed Alissa. "But you're not boring!"

"I'm glad to hear that," said Balin. "Because we still have much to do today. And you need to listen carefully."

Alissa took her place near the wizard's chair. She paid close attention as Balin talked of spells for bringing rain.

Alissa loved the time she spent in Balin's tower. She'd been the wizard's student for several months—since shortly after her tenth birthday.

Sometimes Alissa thought that Balin was the best-kept secret in the kingdom. Only two other people seemed to know about the wizard. And about Alissa's visits to his tower in the far corner of the castle.

One of those people was Alissa's father, King Edmund. As a boy, the king had studied with Balin too. He trusted the wizard to help Alissa learn how to be a good queen.

The other person who knew was Lia. She was Alissa's best friend and lady-in-waiting. The first time the princess went to Balin's tower, Lia had been with her. Sometimes Lia still came along for a lesson. But usually Alissa studied alone with Balin.

Balin finished reading. He closed his book and handed it to Alissa. "I've marked a spell for you to practice," the wizard said. "And now you'd better be going. Didn't you come here early this afternoon because you have to meet with Sir Drear?"

"That's right," said Alissa. "Lia and I are having our history lesson in the portrait gallery. She's waiting for me there."

"And is she complaining about her lessons too?" the wizard asked.

"You know that Lia never complains," sighed Alissa. "I think she likes learning history from dull Sir Drear and manners from my fussy great-aunts."

Then Alissa looked at the wizard. "You asked about Lia because you think I complain too much, didn't you?"

Balin smiled. "Do you, princess?"

"Perhaps." Alissa grinned.

"Now off with you," said the wizard. "And keep an open mind, Alissa. You may actually learn something interesting from Sir Drear."

"I doubt it," said Alissa. "But I'll try."

At the door, she stopped and glanced up. Bartok, Balin's parrot, sat high overhead. Alissa had learned to wait for his crabby good-bye.

"Begone!" squawked the parrot.

"Good-bye to you too, Bartok," the princess called. Then she pulled open the door and headed down the twisting steps. Before long she had crossed the courtyard and entered the castle.

~

"There you are!" said Lia. "I was afraid you'd be late. And you know that makes Sir Drear cross."

"Sir Drear is always cross," said Alissa. "Do you think all stewards are like that?"

Lia laughed. "Well, running a kingdom is hard work. But I think he may be crabbier than most."

Lia got up from the bench where she'd been waiting. Together the girls walked through the arched doorway that led to the portrait gallery.

The gallery was really a hallway that connected two parts of the castle. Several long, narrow windows were cut into the walls. And in the spaces between these windows hung paintings of all sizes.

Lia walked slowly through the gallery, studying the portraits. But Alissa stopped at a window. She gazed longingly at the sunlit gardens below.

"I don't see why Sir Drear needs to show us the portraits," she said. "I've been coming here since I was small. It's not like anything ever changes. Just walls filled with paintings of people dead long ago. Every one of them sad and gloomy too."

"Maybe you haven't been looking carefully then," said Lia. "Because *he* certainly isn't sad or gloomy."

Alissa quickly joined Lia. Her friend was standing in front of a portrait of an elderly man. He was gray-haired and gray-eyed. His lips were turned up in a warm smile. And there was a friendly gleam in his eyes.

"I've never seen this portrait before!" said Alissa in surprise. She checked the nameplate on the wooden frame.

"'Sir Grendon,'" she read. "I haven't heard of him either. Well, you're right, Lia. He doesn't look gloomy. He looks like someone I'd want to know."

At the sound of footsteps, both girls moved away from the portrait. Sir Drear had arrived. Alissa and Lia watched as the tall, bony steward approached. His head was down, and he was reading some papers he had in his hands.

Alissa sighed. It was time to listen to Drear go on and on about the kingdom's history. He especially liked to talk about his own ancestors. Drear felt that every one of them had played an important part in Arcadia's past.

When he reached the girls, Sir Drear looked up. As usual, his thin lips formed a straight line across his gray face.

But instead of beginning the lesson, the steward dropped his papers. A shocked look washed over his face. Then two large spots of red appeared on his cheeks.

Slowly Drear raised a shaking hand and pointed toward Alissa. In a loud voice he cried, "What is the meaning of that?"

CHAPTER TWO

Who Is Sir Grendon?

lissa drew back. What was Sir Drear so upset about? Did she still have blue powder on her dress? Or had she done something wrong?

Then she realized that Drear wasn't looking at her. He was staring past her—right at the portrait of Sir Grendon!

"I don't know what it's doing here, Sir Drear," said Alissa. "But I did want to ask you about him. Who is he? And why haven't I ever seen his portrait before?"

"You've never seen his portrait before because it doesn't belong here!" cried Drear. "The very idea..." he added in a low voice. The red spots on his cheeks grew even redder.

Then Sir Drear glanced back at his students. Both were staring at him in wonder. Quickly the steward tried to pull himself together. His face settled into its usual serious lines. "Come, princess. And you too, Lia. It's time to begin our tour."

Sir Drear headed for the far end of the hall. Lia glanced at Alissa, who just shook her head in amazement. The two girls followed the steward.

Before long Alissa found herself fighting yawns. At each portrait, Drear would unwind a lengthy tale about that person. A great many dates and documents with long names seemed to be part of every story.

Pausing before an unusually gloomy man, Drear said with

pride, "This was my father, Sir Thaddeus, steward before me."

Alissa peered at the picture. Yes, she could see the likeness. Same gray skin. Same serious face. Same bony body.

After hearing about Thaddeus and several others, they finally reached Sir Grendon. Alissa couldn't wait to hear what Sir Drear had to say about him. But Drear passed right by.

"Excuse me, Sir Drear," she said. "You forgot to tell us about Sir Grendon."

"There is nothing to tell, your majesty," said Drear coldly. "As I said before, this portrait shouldn't even be here."

Drear moved the girls along to the next painting. He talked so steadily that Alissa didn't have a chance to ask more questions.

In fact, Alissa was beginning to think that Drear would talk until dinner. Luckily the arrival of a young page brought the lesson to a stop.

"Pardon me, Sir Drear," said the boy. "A messenger just arrived. He brings word from King Edmund. Something about preparing for next week's Court of Justice."

"Very well," said Drear. He bowed to Alissa and Lia. "I am sorry that I have to leave now. But with your father away, princess, there is much I must do."

"That's all right, Sir Drear," said Alissa. "We'll finish studying the portraits by ourselves."

The two girls watched as Sir Drear marched off behind the page. Once they were alone, Alissa turned to Lia. "There's some mystery about this Grendon," she said.

"Mystery?" Lia repeated. "Just because Sir Drear won't talk about him?"

"Not just that," Alissa replied. "But why won't he? And where did the portrait come from? That's the real mystery."

She tapped her foot as she thought. Then she turned to Lia. "I'm going to find out more about Sir Grendon."

Lia looked interested but a bit worried. "Aren't you afraid that will make Sir Drear angry?"

"I won't ask *him* any more questions," Alissa said. "And I'll be so careful that he'll never know what I'm doing. I've got a good idea of just where to start too."

"Where?" Lia asked.

"With someone who must look at these portraits every day. Tell me, Lia, who usually dusts the gallery?"

"That's Gerty's job," replied Lia.

"Good," said Alissa. "Gerty loves to talk. She'll tell us how this picture got into the gallery. Let's find her right now."

"Now? But it's almost time for dinner," objected Lia. "And Lady Matilda will notice if we're not seated on time."

That brought Alissa up short. Great-aunt Matilda wouldn't be happy if they were late. But the princess just couldn't wait!

"Then we'll have to hurry," said Alissa. "Let's go."

After a quick search of the hallways, the two girls found Gerty. She was busily dusting a suit of armor.

"Gerty!" Alissa called. "I've got to ask you something!"

"Me?" Gerty said in surprise. "Well, ask away then."

"You dust the portrait gallery every day, don't you?"

"That I do," replied Gerty. Then she looked worried. "Is Lady Matilda complaining about my work again?"

"No, no," Alissa said. "I just wondered if you'd noticed who hung the portrait of Sir Grendon."

"Sir who?" asked Gerty.

"Grendon," repeated Alissa. "A kind-looking old man with gray hair."

"I wouldn't know, milady," said Gerty. "I don't really study the paintings that closely. Anyway, they all look much the same to me. All neat and proper and...well...dead."

"I don't suppose anyone else might know?" asked Alissa.

Gerty gave her a helpful smile. "You could ask Sir Drear," she suggested. "He's the one who decides which pictures get hung. Besides, there's not much he doesn't notice."

Alissa sighed deeply. "I know."

Lia quickly added, "Thank you for the help, Gerty." Then she tugged on Alissa's arm. "It's time we went to dinner."

As they started down the hall, Alissa paused. "Let's go through the gallery again. I want another look at the portrait."

"All right," agreed Lia. "If we're quick about it."

In the gallery, the two girls returned to the portrait. "If only Sir Grendon could talk," Alissa said.

As the princess leaned forward, a shadow fell across the surface of the picture. She spun around. Had Sir Drear come back?

But there was no one behind them.

"That's strange," said Alissa in a low voice. "Did you see that shadow, Lia?"

"Yes," her friend answered. "Maybe it was just a cloud."

"Maybe," Alissa said slowly. Though she noted that there was hardly a cloud in the sky.

Alissa shrugged and turned back to the portrait. As she studied the painting, her interest grew. Grendon stood in front of an open door that was partly blocked by a tapestry. The heavy cloth was a bright purple and gold. Its design was one of roaring lions and rearing unicorns.

Strange, thought Alissa. Lions and unicorns stood for the kings and queens of Arcadia. But she didn't remember any bright purple-and-gold tapestries in the castle. And as her great-aunts always said: "One never throws away a tapestry. With proper care, they should outlast your children's children's children." Well, surely that went as far back as Grendon.

But what really caught Alissa's attention were two small objects. One was the key that Grendon held in his hand. It looked like he was inviting her to take it. The other was a small golden chest that sat on the floor. Jewels surrounded what appeared to be a keyhole.

Alissa pointed to the portrait. "Do you see that key?" she asked. "And the chest on the floor? The key must unlock the door or the chest—or both. But I don't remember seeing any of those things in the castle. Where could they be?"

Alissa turned to Lia, her face bright with excitement. "More mysteries! I can't wait to begin solving them!"

CHAPTER THREE

Unladylike Questions

Outside the door of her great-aunts' chamber, Alissa stopped and took a deep breath. Then she gently knocked. She and Lia were on time this morning—but just barely. Alissa had overslept. It had been a restless night filled with dreams of lions and unicorns and strange tapestries.

"Enter!" barked a voice from the other side. Great-aunt Matilda didn't sound like she was in the best of moods.

Stepping inside the room, Alissa took a quick look at her tall, thin great-aunt. Matilda wore her straight gray hair pulled back into a net of the same shade. She was never a very cheerful sight, and today was no exception. Matilda stood with her arms folded across her chest, a frown on her face. But Alissa saw that, for once, the frown wasn't aimed at her.

Instead, Matilda was staring at her younger sister. Short, plump Great-aunt Maude sat on a footstool. Soft white hair curled about her rosy face. At the moment, her pale blue eyes looked confused. After seeing the mess of yarn in Maude's lap, Alissa could guess why.

"That's enough, Maude," snapped Matilda. "You will only make things worse. Just leave that yarn for a serving maid to deal with."

As usual Maude made no reply. She rarely said anything

that wasn't simply an echo of her sister's words.

Now Matilda turned to Alissa and Lia. "It is past time for us to begin our work," she said. "Today we begin a count of castle goods."

"I remember," said Alissa. Without thinking, she sighed.

"Now, Alissa," said Matilda. "None of that. You will be queen of Arcadia one day. And, of course, you will want the castle to run smoothly. As queen, you will not have to count things yourself. But you should know what to expect of those who do."

Then Matilda picked up a ring of keys and started out the door. "Come, girls—and Maude," she ordered. "We shall go to the linen storeroom first."

Alissa followed, but her mind wasn't on linens. The sight of Matilda's keys reminded her of the key in Grendon's portrait.

As they made their way down the hall, Alissa leaned toward Lia. "I'll bet the great-aunts know something about Grendon," she whispered.

"What do you mean?" Lia whispered back.

"They're so old! I'm sure they were around in Grendon's day, even if they were just girls. They must remember him!"

Alissa sped up until she was walking beside Matilda.

"Great-aunt," Alissa said in her most ladylike voice, "do you mind if I ask a question?"

"Very well," said Matilda without slowing.

"Can you tell me anything about Sir Grendon?" Alissa asked.

Matilda came to a sudden stop. Poor Maude, who was following close behind, crashed right into her sister.

"Sir Grendon?" asked Matilda as she untangled herself from Maude.

"Sir Grendon?" echoed Maude.

"Yes," said Alissa. "I saw his portrait in the gallery. And I'd like to know more about him."

"Sir Grendon," Maude said once again in a soft voice. She sounded as if she were going to say more. But when Matilda gave her a sharp look, Maude's mouth snapped shut.

"There is nothing to tell you," Matilda said coldly. She started down the hall again. "And you must be mistaken, Alissa. That man's portrait would never hang in the gallery."

"But it *is* there, Great-aunt," Alissa said. "Isn't it, Lia?"

"That's right, Lady Matilda. I saw it myself," replied Lia.

Matilda stopped once more and swung around to face the two girls. "Sir Grendon was a disgrace. He is not to be spoken of in this castle," she said in a low voice.

"But—" began Alissa.

"That's quite enough, Alissa," said Matilda firmly. "It is unladylike to ask unwanted questions."

Alissa gave up. Once Matilda decided that something was "unladylike," there was no changing her mind.

They went on in silence to the room where the castle linens were stored. Matilda unlocked the door. Then she set Alissa and Lia to counting.

"How many tablecloths?" Matilda asked.

"Ten," answered Lia. Matilda carefully wrote the number in her record book.

"And how many coverlets?" she asked Alissa.

Alissa jerked to attention. "Coverlets? Oh yes. They're right here."

"I know they *are* here, Alissa," said Matilda. "What I want to know is *how many* are here."

Alissa sighed. "I'm sorry. I was thinking of something else. I guess I lost count." She tried to pay better attention after that.

When they finished with the linens, the four moved on to the candlemaker's workroom. By the time they were done counting candles, Alissa's fingers were coated with wax.

After that Matilda declared, "Now we must check the spice supply in the kitchen."

More counting! Alissa was tired of numbers. But at least they were headed for the kitchen.

Alissa had done much of her growing up in the castle kitchen. Her mother had died when she was just a baby. Although her father was wonderful, he *was* king—and very busy. So Alissa had found comfort and attention in the warm kitchen. And from kind, good-hearted Cook. It was Cook who'd cared for Alissa's bumps and scratches and listened to her adventures.

These days Alissa didn't have much time to spend in the kitchen. Still, Cook was one of her favorite people.

When they arrived, Cook was stirring a fat kettle that hung over the fire. She smiled at the sight of Alissa and Lia.

"Well, it's a fine thing to have visitors," Cook exclaimed in a loud, cheerful voice. Matilda frowned at the noise.

"Yes, very good," she said sharply. "We're here to check the spice supply."

"I'll not stand in your way, ladies," said Cook. "I know it's important work you're doing." She winked at Alissa and Lia.

Matilda unlocked a storeroom and put the girls to work once more. As Alissa counted bottles and packets of spice, she breathed deeply. The sweet scents of cinnamon and nutmeg mixed with the sharp smell of cloves.

"It makes me think of Cook's gingerbread," Alissa said to Lia. "And that makes me hungry."

"You're not the only one," said Lia. She pointed to the kitchen table. There sat Maude. Alissa's great-aunt was listening to Cook and eating a big slice of cake.

Alissa laughed. "Do you think Great-aunt Matilda knows that one of her helpers is missing?" she asked.

A loud voice answered that question. "Maude!" cried Matilda.

With a guilty look, Maude jumped up. She quickly tried to brush the cake crumbs from her face and dress.

"That will do for today, girls," Matilda announced. She locked the spice door and pocketed the key. Then she herded her sister out of the kitchen.

16

Alissa smiled happily. "I guess we're free now," she said. "May we stay and visit?"

"Of course," said Cook. "And you'll be wanting some cake too, I suppose." The girls nodded.

"So what have you been doing lately?" Cook asked as Alissa and Lia ate. "Besides counting things, I mean."

"We've been studying Arcadia's past," said Lia.

"That's right," added Alissa. "Kings and queens. Births and marriages. Wars and peace treaties. And lots and lots of dates."

Alissa took another bite of cake. Then she swallowed quickly as a thought struck her. "Cook, you know everything that goes on in the castle."

"That I do," said Cook proudly. "There's not much news that doesn't make its way to my kitchen."

"So you can tell us about the portrait," Alissa said.

"And what portrait is that?" asked Cook.

"The one that just appeared in the gallery," replied Alissa. "The portrait of Sir Grendon."

Cook's spoon slipped out of her hand and into the kettle. Slowly she turned and stared at Alissa.

"Sir Grendon, you say?" she asked.

Then, for the third time that day, Alissa heard the same warning. And in the same chilly voice. Only this time, it was coming from Cook.

"That's not a subject you should be talking about, princess. You can't imagine what trouble Grendon's name can stir up!"

CHAPTER FOUR

The Scandal

 ut Cook—" Alissa began.

"No, Alissa," Cook said firmly. "No more about Sir Grendon." She seemed to shiver just a bit. Then she went back to stirring her kettle.

Alissa and Lia looked at each other. In silence they finished their cake. As they got up to leave, Cook called out to Alissa. "Don't let that curiosity of yours get the better of you," she warned. She returned to her work before the princess could answer.

Alissa was quiet until they were well out of the kitchen. "I don't understand," she said to Lia. "I expect Sir Drear and Great-aunt Matilda to be impatient with my questions. But Cook..."

"I agree," said Lia. "Cook usually loves to tell what she knows."

"There's something mysterious about Sir Grendon," Alissa said. "Great-aunt Matilda tells me the man is a disgrace. And then Cook acts frightened at the mention of his name. They only make me more curious. I have to find out what's going on."

So she began asking questions. And more questions. By the middle of the next day, Alissa had talked to almost all of the old-timers in the castle. But she hadn't learned much. In fact, when she mentioned Grendon's name, even the most talkative souls became silent.

"I'm running out of people to ask," Alissa told Lia later. "If only my father weren't away right now. I'm sure he'd know about Grendon. And he'd tell me too."

"Well, you've still got one person left. Though he might just say you should mind your own business," said Lia.

"You mean Balin, don't you?" Alissa asked.

Lia nodded.

Alissa thought about that. "I'll do it. After all, learning about the kingdom's past *is* my business."

Later Alissa reported for her lesson with the wizard. She didn't ask about Grendon at once. She had decided to wait until just the right moment. Not that she had any idea when that moment might be.

"Today you're going to try a spell for making the wind blow," announced Balin. He handed Alissa a large book. "Read the marked page and begin when you're ready," he instructed. Then he went back to studying his crystal ball.

Alissa read the spot that Balin had marked. The spell seemed easy—and fun.

"First I need a piece of string," she said to herself. "One as long as my shadow."

Alissa walked over to a window where the sun made its way into the tower. She twirled in the light, looking for her shadow.

"There it is," said Alissa. Then she remembered that she needed string. She went to a shelf and took down a ball of string and some scissors.

Alissa returned to the patch of sunlight. Carefully she stepped on the very tip of the string. Then she unwound the string until it reached over her head. At this time of day, Alissa's shadow was even taller than she was.

When the length of shadow and string matched, Alissa cut off the piece.

"Now I'm ready to begin," she said to herself. She took her string and book of spells and sat on the rug near Balin.

"Let's see," Alissa said. "Next I'm supposed to tie knots in the string."

"Remember to read the instructions carefully," Balin reminded her.

"I will," promised Alissa. She tied a knot at one end of the string. Then she looked up at the wizard.

"Balin, may I ask you a question?" she said.

"Of course." Balin seemed surprised that Alissa had asked permission. She usually filled their time together with questions.

"You know I'm studying Arcadian history," Alissa said.

Balin nodded. "Is this a question about history?" he asked.

"Yes," said Alissa, her fingers busy tying knots. "You've lived in this tower since my great-grandfather's time. So I decided you were a good person to ask."

"I'm glad that my age makes me so useful," said Balin. "What is your question?"

"What do you know about Sir Grendon?" she asked.

"Sir Grendon!" Balin drew back a little. "Hmmm. Where did you hear about him?"

"His portrait was in the gallery when Lia and I had our lesson there," she answered. "And no one will tell me about him. Except to say that he was a disgrace. So will you tell me? Please?"

"I'm not surprised that no one will talk to you of

Grendon," Balin said. "I'm sure that Drear has warned everyone to keep silent. But I'm also sure that you won't rest until you have some answers. So I'll tell you what I can."

When he saw Alissa's excited look, Balin held up a hand in warning. "Keep in mind that I know only what I've been told. I wasn't even here in Arcadia at the time of the scandal."

Alissa dropped the string. "Scandal?" she cried. "What scandal? What horrible thing did Grendon do? And why were you gone?"

"Don't forget your magic lesson," ordered the wizard. "Continue with your work while I tell the story."

The wizard stared off into the distance as he began the tale. "Grendon was steward of Arcadia for many years."

"Steward!" repeated Alissa. "But doesn't that mean—"

"Yes," said Balin. "That means he's an ancestor of Sir Drear. In fact, Grendon was Drear's grandfather."

Alissa shook her head in wonder. "Grandfather! Why, they're nothing alike. Grendon looks so kind and friendly. While Drear..." She trailed off.

"Grendon is probably one reason why Drear is so serious," said Balin. "Drear feels that his grandfather brought great shame to their family. Yet at first, Grendon was thought to be a good steward. A good man too. But then a terrible plague reached Arcadia."

Alissa shivered. She'd heard stories of the plague. The deadly illness struck out of the blue and killed just as quickly.

"Many in the kingdom were dying," the wizard continued. "Not even my magic was of any help. Then King Garrick, your great-grandfather, called me to him. He asked me to visit a mighty sorcerer who lived far away. I agreed to go. I hoped that together our powers might stop the spread of the plague."

"And were you able to?" asked Alissa.

Balin only shook his head. The look in his eyes told Alissa that his memories were painful.

"While I was gone, both the king and queen became ill." Balin's voice shook. "Nothing could be done for them. First the queen died. And soon after, so did the king."

"Oh, Balin," said Alissa. "How sad."

"Yes," said Balin. "It was a sad time for Arcadia in many ways. And Grendon bore some of the blame."

"But why?" asked the princess.

"I only know what I could piece together later," said the wizard. "By the time I'd heard of the king's death and returned, Grendon was gone."

"Gone!" echoed the princess. "Did he die of the plague too?"

"No," said Balin. "But many people said he was afraid he might die. So afraid that he left Arcadia. He deserted his dying king, his country, and his family. Worse yet, the new king—your grandfather—was just a boy."

Alissa nodded. "I know about that. Grandfather was only six when he became king."

"Yes," nodded Balin. "Far too young to rule a kingdom alone. And then it was discovered that King Garrick had left no will. Which meant no one had been named as regent to guide the new king."

The wizard sighed. "That was Baron Mendor's chance. He was a truly evil, power-hungry man. Mendor took over as regent, claiming that the old king had asked him to do so. Many people didn't believe him. But Grendon was the only one who might have stopped the baron. And he was gone."

Balin fell silent. Then he softly added, "You know that I

never interfere with the workings of the kingdom. But this was one time I was greatly tempted to do so. Fortunately the baron died before he could bring Arcadia to ruin."

Balin rose. "Well, that's enough about Grendon. If you're ready, Alissa, let's see if you can make the wind blow."

Alissa tore her thoughts away from Balin's story. She again studied the words of the spell. Then she stood up with the string in her hands. She untied the first knot as she spoke:

> For each knot I untie,
> Stir the wind in the sky.

As the knot came apart, a puff of wind blew through the tower. Balin's heavy white beard moved in the breeze.

"It worked!" cried Alissa in excitement.

"Continue," said Balin.

Quickly Alissa untied knot after knot. As each came loose, a great gust of wind swept through the room. And each gust was stronger than the last. Papers began to fly about. The wizard's hat blew off his head. High overhead, Bartok squawked in fright as his perch swayed wildly.

"STOP!" shouted Balin.

Alissa was so surprised that she dropped the string. At once the wind died down. Papers slowly drifted to the floor—as did a few of Bartok's feathers.

"Alissa," said Balin with a frown. "How many knots did the instructions say to make?"

"Let me check," said Alissa. She opened the book, which had blown shut, and found the spell.

"Three," she said in a small voice.

"And how many did you tie?"

asked Balin.

"A lot," admitted Alissa. "Oh, Balin, your story was so interesting. I just lost track of what I was doing. I'm sorry."

The wizard snorted. "Really! I've told you before, Alissa. If you want to learn magic, you must follow instructions."

"I guess I'm done for today?" she asked.

"Quite done, princess," said Balin.

But before leaving, Alissa had one more question.

"I still don't see why Drear won't let anyone talk about Grendon," she said. "Why should something that happened so long ago matter?"

"Think about it, Alissa," the wizard replied. "You know how proud Drear is of his family's long history of serving Arcadia. Can't you see why he wouldn't want to talk about his grandfather? Someone who turned his back on his family, king, and country?"

"I suppose so," said Alissa slowly. "But what's past is past."

"Not to Sir Drear," said the wizard with a sigh. "So please let the matter rest now."

Thinking about Balin's words, Alissa absent-mindedly fingered the string. She didn't realize that she'd untied another knot until a puff of wind slammed the door shut behind her.

"Begone!" came Bartok's angry squawk.

CHAPTER FIVE

A Key Clue

rooster crowed in the courtyard. Alissa groaned and pulled the covers over her head.

"Get up, lazybones," called Lia. She poked her head in from her own room next door.

Uncovering one eye, Alissa peeked out at Lia. Her friend was already dressed.

Alissa sat up in bed. "Lia, I've been lying here and thinking. Why did Sir Grendon turn into such a coward?"

Lia wrinkled her nose. "I don't know. And I'm not sure you'll ever find an answer to that question." Then she asked, "So have you decided what you'll do next?"

There was a long silence. Finally Alissa said, "I'm going to take Balin's advice. No more questions about Sir Grendon. I think I know all I want to about him."

Lia stared at her friend in surprise. It wasn't like Alissa to give up on something—no matter who suggested doing so.

"That's a good idea," she said. "And now you really should get dressed, Alissa."

The princess crawled out of bed. A serving girl had already quietly come and gone. Alissa's clothing was neatly laid out. And steam rose from a pitcher of hot water atop her nightstand.

Alissa reached for the pitcher. As she did every morning,

she poured the water into her washing bowl.

Clink!

Alissa stared in surprise. Then she called, "Lia! Look at this!"

Lia rushed over to the nightstand. At the bottom of the bowl was a large key.

"How on earth did that get there?" asked Lia.

Alissa fished the key out of the water. "Do you know what this is? This is the key that Grendon was holding in the portrait!"

"Grendon!" said Lia. "Alissa, just a minute ago you said you'd had enough of him! Besides, it may look like the same key, but how could it be? Grendon has been dead for ages!"

"Well, this key changes everything. Don't you see how strange it is that I found it my water pitcher? And I'll prove to you that it's the same key. We'll go to the gallery and look at the portrait again."

Alissa quickly dressed and led the way back to the gallery. She rushed to the spot where Grendon's portrait hung.

But the portrait was no longer there. In its place was a painting of an old knight on an even older horse.

"Where is it?" Alissa cried. She ran to the end of the gallery, checking every portrait.

"It's gone!" she groaned at last.

"Do you suppose Sir Drear took it?" asked Lia.

"That must be it," said Alissa. "Let's go ask."

"Ask Sir Drear?" cried Lia.

"No, of course not," answered Alissa. "We'll ask Gerty again."

But a check with Gerty told them nothing. She hadn't moved the portrait. Neither had any of the other servants in that part of the castle.

"Drear must have moved it himself," Alissa said finally. "I'll bet he put it in the accounts room. No one else ever goes in there. But I'm going to!"

"Alissa!" exclaimed Lia. "You wouldn't dare!"

"Yes, I would," replied the princess. "At least I will if you'll stand guard."

So Lia found herself sitting on a bench near the accounts room. She seemed to be busy with a piece of embroidery. But her eyes were on the hallway, not on her work.

Meanwhile, Alissa let herself into the room. She turned slowly, peering into the shadows. "Let me think," she said to herself. "Where would he have hidden the portrait?"

Alissa set off on a search. She lifted tapestries from the wall. She peered under the heavy cloth that covered Drear's worktable. She moved books and papers. But she didn't find the portrait.

"If it's not here, I don't know where he would have put it," Alissa whispered. She studied the room once more.

"I may as well look for other clues," she said. She went over to Drear's shelves. Tall books and rolled documents covered every inch.

"Let's see. Grendon's papers wouldn't be near the top of the pile." She unrolled documents and rooted through papers. She found nothing about Grendon, however.

"Where else?" Alissa said softly. Then an idea hit her. "The account books!" she cried. "Those are kept forever. So some of them must have been Sir Grendon's."

She found the books on a high shelf. Quickly she lifted

one down and began flipping through the pages. But they told her nothing about Grendon. They were simply filled with rows of numbers written in a fine hand.

Just as she replaced the book, Alissa heard a voice outside. Was it Lia?

"Good morning, Sir Drear."

It *was* Lia! And she was talking to Drear! The steward was at the door!

Wildly Alissa looked around. Where to hide?

The worktable! Alissa darted underneath it, pulling the cloth into place again. And just in time! The door opened.

"Good day to you then, sir," she heard Lia say cheerfully.

"Hmmm, yes," replied Drear. He shut the door firmly behind him.

From her hiding place, Alissa heard Drear walk past. Then he sank into the chair next to the table. His large, narrow feet suddenly appeared beside her own. And his bony knees jutted just inches from Alissa's nose. She held her breath.

The scratching sound of a quill pen followed. Oh no! thought Alissa. He's working on the accounts. He'll be here forever!

Worst of all, Alissa's nose began to itch. She knew she was going to sneeze!

A knock on the door made her forget her itchy nose. Drear pushed his chair back. "Now what?" he sighed. The door opened, and Alissa heard the welcome sound of Lia's voice.

"Forgive me for bothering you, Sir Drear," Lia said. "I think I heard a page calling your name at the other end of the hall."

"Very well. It seems that I'm to have no peace as long as King Edmund is away."

Alissa heard the door close. She didn't dare stick her head out from under the table. Not until she was sure Drear wasn't coming back. Finally she heard the door open again.

"Alissa!" hissed Lia. "Where are you?"

Alissa crawled out from under the table. She gave Lia a smile. "Thanks for saving me."

Lia stamped her foot. "Hurry up. We have to get out of here." She didn't say another thing until they were back in Alissa's chamber. Then she faced the princess, hands on her hips.

"Don't you ever do anything like that again," she ordered.

"I'm sorry," Alissa said. A smile tugged at her lips. "You know, just now you remind me of Great-aunt Matilda."

Lia tried to keep a frown on her face. But she couldn't do it. "I'm beginning to understand why Lady Matilda gets angry at you," she said with a laugh.

"Anyway, thanks for warning me," said Alissa. "And for getting Sir Drear out of the room. I was afraid I'd be trapped there for hours."

"Did you find the portrait?" asked Lia.

Alissa frowned. "No. And that's another mystery. If it's not there, where is it?"

"Surely Sir Drear could just stick it in some old storage room," Lia said.

Alissa shook her head. "Not if he didn't want it found again. Remember, Great-aunt Matilda has the keys to almost every room in the castle."

"Well, we don't," said Lia. "So I think that brings your search to an end."

Alissa paced up and down as she thought about her next move. Suddenly she brightened. "Let's go and visit Cook," she suggested.

"Alissa, you know that Cook won't tell us anything either," Lia said.

"Just watch," replied Alissa. "She'll never be able to keep quiet when she hears what's been going on."

The girls hurried downstairs and made their way to the huge kitchen. When they arrived, they found Cook making bread. A ball of dough lay on the table before her.

"Bread!" cried Alissa. "Oh, Cook, can we help?"

"Surely you can," replied Cook. "But first cover your clothing, ladies."

Alissa and Lia put aprons on and set to work.

"I love the smell of bread dough," said Alissa happily.

"It's a fine smell," agreed Cook. "But the mess is another matter," she said with a glance at Alissa.

"Cook is right," said Lia. "Your whole face is covered with flour."

"So is yours," said Alissa. She finished shaping her piece of dough and wiped her hands. Then she reached into the small bag she kept tied to her belt.

"Cook," she said, "I found something today. Have you ever seen this before?" she asked as she held up the key.

"I can't say that I have," Cook replied. "It looks very old, Alissa. Where did you find it?"

"It was strange," Alissa said in a low, quiet voice. "The key mysteriously appeared in my water pitcher this morning."

"That *is* strange," agreed Cook.

"It's even odder than you might think," Alissa continued. "Oh?"

"This key is the very one that Sir Grendon is holding in his portrait," said Alissa.

Cook's mouth dropped open. "What?" she cried. She added weakly, "We shouldn't be talking of Grendon."

"There's more," Alissa quickly added. "The portrait...?"

Cook nodded slowly.

"Well, it's disappeared," Alissa whispered. "Vanished into thin air! I think—"

She broke off when Cook sat down with a thud. The older woman's floury hand went to her heart. "Oh, me!" she cried. "Keys that appear. Pictures that disappear. I feared this would happen, and now it has."

"What is it? What's happened?" Alissa asked.

"It's Sir Grendon!" cried Cook. "His ghost has come back to haunt us!"

CHAPTER SIX

A Mess of Magic

is ghost!" exclaimed Alissa.

"Cook, are you sure?" Lia asked.

"All too sure," Cook replied in a shaking voice. "Oh, Alissa, I told you to leave it alone. Talking about Grendon, digging up the past. Why, you've stirred up that awful man's ghost again."

"Again! What do you mean?" asked Alissa.

"There have been tales about him before," whispered Cook. "Stories of mysterious happenings. Some even say they've seen the old man walking the halls late at night."

Alissa shivered with excitement. "Have you seen the ghost yourself?"

Cook shivered too—but not with excitement. "No, bless my stars! But just the other evening, I came into the kitchen to check the fires. You know I like to keep a small flame going all night. Well, as I came in, the fire suddenly blazed up! And then I saw a strange shadow on the wall. But there was no one in the kitchen with me."

Alissa's eyes met Lia's. A strange shadow! Just like the one that had fallen across Grendon's portrait in the gallery. It had to be the shadow of the ghost himself!

Cook went on. "Now you tell me of this key. And portraits that appear and disappear. So listen to me, Alissa. And listen

33

well this time. Lay this matter to rest. Stop bothering the ghost."

"Bothering him?" objected Alissa. "How am I bothering him?"

"All these questions," said Cook. "Maybe he wants the matter forgotten."

"Maybe he wants someone to stir things up," Alissa shot back.

Then the princess realized that Cook was truly upset. She patted the woman's broad shoulder. "Don't worry. I won't do anything to make him angry."

Cook smacked her spoon on the table. "It's stubborn you are, my girl. Well, you'd better not let your great-aunts know of these doings. The old ladies will faint dead away if they find you're chasing ghosts. For the last time, Alissa, leave it alone."

"But it won't leave *me* alone," Alissa gently replied. "I think Sir Grendon wants me to find out about him."

Cook just shook her head.

The girls were silent as they left the kitchen and headed upstairs.

When they got back to Alissa's chamber, Lia turned to her friend. "Alissa, I'm not sure I believe that there's really a ghost in the castle. But maybe Cook is right. Maybe you should forget about Sir Grendon."

"I can't," Alissa insisted. "I know he's the one who made the key appear. And perhaps the portrait too. So he must want me to do something!

"Besides," she added, "I'm supposed to be learning magic. Why shouldn't I find out about ghosts?"

So that very afternoon, at the end of her lesson, Alissa brought up the subject. "Balin," she began, "what can you tell me about ghosts?"

"Ghosts?" said Balin. "Why do you want to know?"

In a rush of words, Alissa told him what Cook had said.

Balin listened quietly. When he spoke, his voice was serious. "Few people truly see ghosts. Such sights are usually the result of an overly full stomach or an empty mind."

"But—" began Alissa.

"A real ghost," Balin continued, "is nothing to fool with. Practice the magic you've been given. And leave Grendon's ghost—if it truly is walking—alone."

With a sigh, Alissa said good-bye and left the wizard's tower.

But by the time she'd reached her chambers, Alissa felt happier. After all, Balin had told her to practice the magic he'd already given her. And she had three of the wizard's books, all filled with spells.

Alissa pulled out the books and curled up on her bed. For a long time, she studied spell after spell.

When Lia came in, Alissa looked up. "Listen to this, Lia. Here's a spell I can use to find out about Sir Grendon."

"What spell is that?" asked Lia.

"One that uses dirt to read the past. It doesn't have to be dirt the person actually stepped on. It just has to be from near a place that person has been."

She shut her book and stared at the wall. "Now where might Grendon have walked?"

"The castle gardens," suggested Lia. "Sir Drear and your father often go out there when they're talking."

"Lia, that's a wonderful idea!" Alissa cried. She leapt from her bed and grabbed the water pitcher from the nightstand. "Let's try it!"

The girls hurried down the stairs and out into the gardens. There Alissa searched for a good spot to dig. At last she knelt down at the edge of a flower bed.

"A little dirt won't be missed from here," she said. Alissa began to dig. But the dirt was hard, and she had only her fingers to use as a tool.

"Oh, bother!" she said. "I should have brought a spoon."

"Will this do?" asked Lia. She handed Alissa a flat stone with a sharp edge.

"Perfect," said Alissa. Using the stone as a scoop, she soon had half a pitcher of dirt.

The princess stood up and wiped her dirty hands on her skirt. "Now we need a stick of ash," she said. Alissa looked around blankly. If only she'd paid attention when Balin told her what ash trees looked like.

Fortunately Lia knew. She broke a small branch off a tree that grew near the fish pond. Then the friends went back inside the castle.

Alissa opened the book again and leaned it against her footstool. Eyes on the page, she emptied the pitcher onto her rug. She spread the dirt out evenly.

"Alissa, are you sure you're doing this right?" asked Lia.

"Yes," her friend replied. Then she looked up. "Well, you're supposed to scatter the dirt on a golden cloth. But I don't have one."

She scrambled to her feet. Holding the tree branch in front of her, Alissa said the words of the spell:

Branch of ash in my hand held fast—
From this dirt, I will read the past.

She stood with the branch in hand, waiting. And waiting. At last she lowered her arm.

"Nothing happened!" Alissa said sadly. She stared at the dirty rug. "And now I have this mess to clean up." She put most of the dirt back into her water pitcher. Then she lifted the rug, carried it to her window, and gave it a shake.

She put the rug back in place and dusted dirt off her hands. "Well," she said, "that seems a poor sort of spell to put in a book."

"Maybe it only works if you follow the instructions exactly," said Lia.

Alissa bit her bottom lip as she thought about that. Then she shrugged and announced, "I'm going to try another spell." She looked through the book again.

"Lia! This is it!" Alissa cried after several minutes of reading. "Here's a spell that can tell you where a found item belongs."

She reached into the bag at her waist and pulled out the key. "I'm sure this key unlocks the door or the chest in the portrait. We'll use this spell to tell us where to find them."

Alissa placed the key on the floor in the middle of the room. "Lia, I'll need your help. This spell takes two people."

Lia looked over Alissa's shoulder as the princess read the directions.

"'Face one another with the found item between you,'" Alissa read. "'Say the words. Then one of you turns to the east. The other to the west. When you turn back again, you will have your answer.'"

So they did just that. But when they were done, the key looked exactly as it had before.

"Witches' warts!" Alissa cried. "Nothing happened! And I did exactly what the instructions said." She picked up the key.

"Wait!" cried Lia. "Something did happen—look!"

Alissa's eyes went to the spot where Lia pointed. An old tapestry on the wall was billowing, as though it was caught in a breeze.

"That's strange," said Alissa. "I wonder..." She reached for the tapestry and lifted one edge. At once the cloth stopped moving. Alissa dropped it against the wall and stared. Now the tapestry just hung there. She lifted the other corner and studied the wall beneath. Then she shook her head slowly.

"There's nothing here," she said, dropping the tapestry back into place. "And I don't see what this has to do with the key anyway. It can't be the tapestry in Grendon's portrait. That one was bright purple and gold. Mine is blue and silver."

"But it *is* strange that it moved just then," Lia said.

"I probably did the wind spell without meaning to," replied Alissa. She pulled the knotted string from her bag. "See, I still have my string."

Alissa stuffed the string and key back into the bag. "I guess I can't do this kind of magic yet," she said. "I'll have to come up with another plan. One that doesn't use magic."

"Well, we'd better finish cleaning up," suggested Lia. "If the serving girl finds your water pitcher full of dirt, she'll tell Lady Matilda."

"You're right," agreed Alissa. "And I don't think I dare dump *it* out the window! We'll take it back to the garden."

The girls went outside again. Alissa turned the pitcher upside down and emptied it. Then she stopped and stared in amazement.

"Lia!" she cried. "Come and look at this! The pile of dirt is moving! It's magical!"

Lia bent down to look. She picked something off the top of the pile. "I don't know how magical it is. But it's certainly strange."

She held her hand out. "See, you've changed the dirt into a whole pile of lizards!" she said.

Alissa stared in wonder at the tiny brown creature in Lia's hand. "So I have," she breathed. "Maybe I should write down exactly what I did."

"That's a good idea," agreed Lia. "You never know when you might need a good supply of lizards!" Fighting back an attack of giggles, they headed inside.

That night, after the castle had settled down to sleep, Alissa lay awake. There were too many things rattling around in her head to let her rest. She thought about Grendon and why his ghost might be walking. She thought about the words of her spells. And she wondered why her magic wouldn't work—just this once.

Finally the princess drifted off into a very sound sleep. She didn't even notice when her tapestry stirred. It billowed once again before settling against the wall.

CHAPTER SEVEN

The Ghost Walks

Alissa stood in the warm afternoon sunlight and looked around the sewing room. She'd spent most of the day hunting for the tapestry, door, and chest that she'd seen in Grendon's portrait. Lia was busy helping the great-aunts prepare for King Edmund's return. So the princess had searched alone.

Alissa headed across the room. Could this be the door in the portrait? She held her breath and pulled the door open. A pile of pillows tumbled out.

Another dead end. This door just led to a storage closet.

"Oh, your majesty!" cried the seamstress. "I should have warned you. Are you all right?"

"I'm fine," said Alissa as she stuffed the pillows back into the closet and closed the door.

When she was done, Alissa asked the same question she'd been asking all day. "So you're sure there's never been a tapestry near this door?"

"Quite sure, your majesty. At least not in all the time I've been here."

The princess frowned. "Well, I'll not bother you anymore." She headed out of the room.

Alissa touched the key, which now hung on a ribbon around her neck. It had to unlock the door or the chest in the portrait. Why else would it have appeared in her water pitcher?

But Alissa was starting to wonder whether the door, chest, or tapestry existed at all. She'd poked her nose into every corner of the castle. And the only thing she'd found was trouble. While backing up to look closely at one door, she'd stepped on Matilda's foot. Then, while peeking through the library door, she'd bumped into Sir Drear.

"I'm going to forget about the portrait for now," she said to herself. "But I think I'll go and talk to Cook one more time. She did say she'd noticed signs of the ghost."

When Alissa reached the kitchen, she found the place in an uproar.

"I haven't seen it since yesterday," cried a kitchen maid. Cook was standing in front of the girl, hands on her hips.

"Then look where it was yesterday," Cook said.

"What's missing?" asked Alissa.

"My best serving spoon," replied Cook. "It vanished into thin air."

"Vanished," repeated Alissa. Just like Sir Grendon's portrait! "Cook," she said, "you don't suppose that the ghost took it?"

"The ghost!" cried the maid. "I want nothing to do with spirits and such!"

"Enough of that, miss!" said Cook. "I'll have no talk of ghosts in my kitchen."

Alissa wasn't sure whether Cook was talking to her or to the serving maid. So when the maid wandered off in search of the spoon, Alissa apologized. "I'm sorry I said that."

Cook shook her head. "I've already warned you about talking of ghosts, Alissa. And it's just been one thing after another today. I don't need any more foolishness."

"What do you mean?" asked Alissa. "What else has been going on?"

"The floors are crawling with nasty little beasts," Cook said. "And that silly girl screams every time one appears."

An uncomfortable thought popped into Alissa's mind. "What do these beasts look like?" she asked.

"Like this!" cried Cook. Bending over, she scooped up a small, wiggling creature.

Alissa swallowed. "It's just a lizard," she said in an offhand way. "I'll take it out to the garden if you like."

Cook handed over the animal. "Tell the horrible thing to stay out there," she said. "Or I'll be turning it into stew!"

Lizard in hand, Alissa stood for a few moments and watched all the activity. She thought about asking Cook whether there had been more signs of a ghost. But then she decided that wouldn't be wise. There was no chance that Cook would answer her question. In fact, she'd probably get angry.

Alissa sighed. Cook looked over at her and said, "Off with you, my girl. I'm sure you've better things to do than roost here among my pots." She softened her words with a smile.

As Alissa turned to leave, Cook added. "And don't forget to take that beast with you."

"It's right here," said Alissa, holding up the lizard.

At that sight, the kitchen maid screamed again. And she dropped the serving spoon, which she'd found at long last.

～

At dinnertime Alissa reported to Lia. "I didn't find any new clues," she whispered. They were sitting side by side at the table, between the great-aunts. "And I've looked almost everywhere."

Matilda overheard. "What are you looking for, Alissa?" she asked.

The princess dropped her eyes to her plate. "Oh, nothing important, Great-aunt," she said.

"Anything you choose not to share cannot be proper table talk," said Matilda.

"Yes. I mean, no," replied Alissa. "You're right, of course." She sat up straighter. Surely dinner would be over soon. Then she could escape from Matilda's watchful eye.

At last Alissa and Lia were able to excuse themselves from the table. They quickly left the room. But at the staircase, Alissa paused. "Let's take a walk in the garden before going to bed," she suggested. She glanced around. Then she whispered to Lia, "Race you!"

She darted off with a laugh. Lia quickly gathered her skirts and followed. But Alissa had a good head start. In fact, she was far ahead by the time she reached a turn in the hallway. She ran around the corner—

And stopped cold. Ahead of her, a misty figure floated down the hall.

"Lia!" Alissa called in a shaky voice. "Look! Look!"

By the time Lia caught up, there was nothing to be seen. "What is it, Alissa?" she asked. "What's wrong?"

"It was the ghost!" Alissa cried, still trembling. "He's gone now, but I saw him! He was heading right down this hall!"

"Alissa," Lia said with a shake of her head. "You have to stop thinking about Sir Grendon. Your imagination is starting to play tricks on you."

"No!" said Alissa firmly. "I saw him, I tell you. He was wearing the same clothing he wore in the portrait, Lia. It was

43

Sir Grendon!"

"Alissa—" Lia began.

"Please," interrupted Alissa. "You've got to believe me! I did see the ghost!"

Lia stared into Alissa's eyes for a few moments. "All right," she said. "I believe you. I don't understand what's going on, but I believe you."

Then she grabbed Alissa's hand. "Now come on," she said. "Ghost or no ghost, a walk in the garden still sounds like a good idea."

And it was. The fresh night air seemed to blow all thoughts of ghosts out of Alissa's head.

But not for long. Later, as Alissa got ready for bed, she came across one of her magic books. Slowly she flipped through the pages. Then a stubborn look came over her face. "Lia!" she called.

Lia stuck her head into the room. "What is it?" she asked.

"I can prove it," Alissa declared. "I can prove that there's a ghost."

Lia's mouth dropped open. "How in the world can you do that?"

"Listen to this," Alissa replied. "The book says that a true ghost leaves no footprints."

"So?" said Lia.

"So tonight we'll set a trap. A trap for footprints!"

"Alissa, are you sure we should?" Lia asked. Then she noted her friend's disappointed face. "All right. Tell me what you want to do."

Quickly Alissa explained her plan. And late that night, the two girls crept downstairs.

Alissa led the way into the kitchen. By the light of her

candle, she found Cook's flour bin. She filled a cup with flour.

"Now we'll sprinkle this on the floor where I saw Sir Grendon," Alissa whispered. "If he comes this way again, we'll know the truth."

"Because he won't leave any footprints," added Lia. "Not if he's really a ghost."

So the girls scattered the flour in the hall. Then they hid out of sight to await the ghost.

It wasn't a comfortable wait. The floor was hard and chilly. Strange rustles and creaks drifted through the night. And only a single ray of moonlight brightened the hall.

"How long do you plan on waiting here?" asked Lia.

"Shhh," ordered Alissa. "He might hear you."

That was enough for Lia. She wasn't sure that a ghost really was walking around the castle. But if there was one, she didn't want it to notice her.

After a while, they got used to the night noises. Alissa and Lia rested their heads against the wall. Just for a moment, they closed their eyes.

Alissa suddenly awoke. Early dawn lit the hallway. Lia was asleep next to her. Where are we? Alissa wondered.

Then she remembered. The ghost! She'd fallen asleep and missed him! Alissa groaned.

At the sound, something moved at the other end of the hallway, where they had sprinkled the flour. Alissa stood and stared. The misty figure she'd seen before had reappeared.

"Lia!" cried Alissa. "Lia, wake up! It's Sir Grendon!" She charged down the hall.

Lia woke up and jumped to her feet. "I see him, Alissa! Or

something!" she cried.

But by the time they both reached the corner, the figure had vanished again.

"He was here," Alissa said. "And he *is* a ghost. Look!" She pointed to the floor in front of them. There wasn't a footprint to be seen in the scattered flour.

"Alissa!"

The girls spun around. The great-aunts were approaching.

"You're up early today," said Matilda with an unusually pleasant look. "Excellent, excellent. As I've often said, a lady must rise early to see to her duties."

Suddenly Matilda noticed Alissa's wrinkled dress and uncombed hair. Her glance went to Lia, who looked equally messy. Finally it went to the flour-covered floor.

"Ladies," Matilda said in a dangerously calm voice. "I'd like an explanation."

"Sorry about the mess, milady," said Lia.

"It's my fault, Great-aunt," Alissa said quickly. "I was the one who came up with the idea."

"Exactly what was your idea?" Matilda asked.

"I thought I could trap a ghost," said Alissa in a small voice.

Matilda's face grew red, and she seemed to swell up before Alissa's eyes. The princess had never seen her great-aunt this angry before.

When Matilda finally spoke, her words were cold and hard. "This ghost business will stop, Alissa. I have heard complaints from some of the servants about your questions. You have upset and frightened them."

Her eyes grew narrower and her frown deeper. "Well, we have all had enough, my fine lady," she continued. "Your

47

father returns today. You may be sure that he will hear about what you've been up to."

Matilda swept past, her skirts raised to avoid the flour. She paused as she rounded the corner. "And I want this mess cleaned up—NOW!" she ordered. With that, she marched off.

Maude trailed along more slowly. As she passed Alissa, she reached out and patted the princess on the arm.

Alissa stared open-mouthed at her quiet great-aunt. She was even more surprised when the old woman gently smiled.

Without a word, Maude dropped her hand and headed off after her sister.

How strange, thought Alissa. It was as though great-aunt Maude felt sorry for her. But that was impossible. Maude never had an idea or feeling that was any different from Matilda's.

Matilda. Alissa remembered her other great-aunt's angry words. The princess glanced down at the messy floor.

"Well, at least I know how to clean this easily," she told Lia.

Alissa reached into her bag and pulled out her string. She untied a knot and said the words of the spell. A wind arose and picked up the dusting of flour.

But Alissa had forgotten how quickly the spell worked. There wasn't time to avoid the little whirlwind. The flour blew into their faces, hair, and clothes before racing out the window.

Lia sighed as she looked at the mess. "Please, Alissa," she begged. "No more magic today."

CHAPTER EIGHT

Not Quite a Door

ater that morning, a page appeared at Alissa's door and made an announcement. "The king has returned, your majesty. He would like to see you in the great hall."

"Very well," said Alissa. "Please tell him I'll be there right away." She nervously smoothed her hair.

"Do you want me to come along?" asked Lia.

Alissa gave her friend a thankful look. "Please."

"Don't worry, Alissa," said Lia. "I'm sure your father will understand."

"I doubt it," said Alissa sadly. "Great-aunt Matilda has probably gone on and on about what a problem I've been."

They walked to the great hall in silence. Just inside the entryway, they paused. At the front of the room, King Edmund was talking to Drear. Neither man had noticed Alissa and Lia come in.

"I'll be right here," Lia promised. She sat on a bench near the entrance.

Alissa stood and watched her father for a moment. Even if he was upset with her, she was happy to have him back.

The princess took a deep breath and straightened her shoulders. It was time to get this over with.

As Alissa moved toward her father, he looked up. "We'll

finish later," he said to Sir Drear.

"Very well, sire," replied Drear. He bowed and made his way out of the room. As he passed Alissa, Drear nodded coolly.

Alissa stopped in front of her father. He studied her for a few moments. When at last he spoke, his voice was calm but firm. "Well, Alissa?"

"It's good to have you home, Father," Alissa said softly.

"It's good to be home," he answered. "In most respects." Alissa's heart sank.

Then King Edmund added, "I think you know what we need to talk about."

"Yes," said Alissa. She lowered her eyes and picked at the embroidery on her skirt.

"Alissa," her father gently said. "Look at me, please."

Alissa slowly raised her eyes to her father's face. He was smiling slightly, but he looked worried. She threw herself at him and felt his arms go around her in a familiar bear hug.

"Oh, Father!" she cried. "I'm sorry. I didn't mean to cause so much trouble."

The king chuckled. "Whether you meant to or not, it appears you've caused plenty. Now sit down and explain things to me."

The words poured out of Alissa. She told her father of the portrait and everyone's refusal to speak of Grendon. She explained about the key and her search for the door and the chest. She even told him about trying to trap the ghost.

Finally Alissa was finished. Her father just sat quietly and looked at her. Then he took her small hand into his large one.

"Alissa," the king said, "you've upset Drear, Matilda, the servants. Even Cook is unhappy with you."

Alissa nodded sadly.

"Your time would be better spent getting ready for the Court of Justice. I want you to know the rules of law. How past kings and queens have judged cases. One day, as queen, you'll have many responsibilities. And one of those responsibilities will be to see that justice is given to the people of Arcadia."

"I know," she said.

"Very well," King Edmund said. "I trust that I'll hear no more complaints. Now back to your studies. I'll see you at dinner tonight."

Alissa bid her father good-bye. As she walked out of the huge room, the princess noticed that Lia was no longer sitting on the bench. Where had she gone?

Then Alissa saw her friend standing in the hallway, motioning wildly.

She hurried to join Lia. "What is it?" Alissa asked.

Lia pulled the princess closer to the great hall's entrance. "You're not going to believe this!" she whispered.

"Believe what?" asked Alissa crossly. She'd been counting on her friend's sympathy. But Lia was acting as if it didn't matter that Alissa had been scolded.

"The tapestry!" said Lia. "I know where it is!"

It took a moment for Lia's words to sink in. "You mean Sir Grendon's tapestry?" asked Alissa in wonder.

"Yes!" cried Lia. "I was looking around while you were talking to your father. And I spotted it! One of the tapestries was billowing. Just like the one in your chamber did. See for yourself!"

Alissa carefully peeked back into the great hall. She stared at the tapestry her friend pointed out.

"I see it," she whispered. "But it's not billowing now. And it's not Grendon's tapestry either. The one in the portrait was bright purple and gold. This one's dull and gray."

"But the pattern, Alissa," Lia protested. "Just look at the pattern!"

Alissa stared harder. Finally she was able to see what Lia meant. "Lions," she breathed. "And unicorns. It *is* the same!"

"Don't you see?" asked Lia. "You were searching for bright colors. But the tapestry is very old. Its colors have faded since the portrait was painted!"

"So if this is the right tapestry..."

Lia finished the sentence for her. "The door must be hidden behind it."

Alissa gazed longingly at the tapestry. "Bother! We can't check now. There will be people in and out of the great hall all day! Especially with the Court of Justice coming up."

"But Alissa, just think," said Lia in an excited voice. "Now we know why the tapestry in your room billowed. It was a sign to look for another one that does the same thing."

"That means my magic worked," said Alissa in wonder. "It really worked!"

She turned to her friend. "We'll have to wait until tonight. And then come back when there's no one here!"

Lia quickly agreed. "All right. Let's go upstairs and make our plans."

So that night, long after everyone had gone to bed, they crept down the stairs. This time Lia led the way into the great hall. There she lit the candles they had brought with them.

"I'll keep watch," offered Lia. "You look."

Lia waited near the entrance of the hall, while Alissa went to check the tapestry. Carefully the princess reached out and lifted a corner. A puff of dust rose up from the cloth. Alissa sneezed loudly and dropped the tapestry back against the wall.

"Shhh!" came Lia's voice.

Again Alissa lifted a corner of the tapestry—higher this time. And there behind it was—

"Toads' toenails!" wailed Alissa. "It's just a blank wall!"

Lia rushed over. Side by side, they stared in silence. There was no sign of a door.

"Drat!" cried Alissa. "I can't believe there's no door here." She kicked the wall angrily.

Immediately she was sorry. "Ouch! That hurt!" She sank to the floor and rubbed her foot.

"Alissa!" Lia exclaimed. She bent over to check her friend's foot. "Well, I don't think you broke it. Can you stand up?"

Alissa sighed. "Yes, I think so," she said. She struggled to her feet, supporting herself against the stone wall.

The wall seemed to move ever so slightly. Alissa pulled her hand back. Then she looked more closely. A long slit had appeared!

She pushed harder. Slowly a piece of the wall opened up and swung back like a door. They could see a dark passageway beyond.

"Glory be!" cried Lia. "There *is* a door!"

"Well, it's not quite a door," said Alissa. "But this passageway must have something to do with Sir Grendon! Maybe it will lead us to the golden chest."

Alissa turned to Lia. "We have to go inside!" she said. Her eyes were shining with excitement.

Lia shivered. Then she picked up her candle and gripped it tightly. "All right. Let's go," she said in a shaky voice.

Alissa's hand trembled a little as she pushed the stone door farther open. But neither girl looked back as they entered the dark passage.

CHAPTER NINE

The Secret Passageway

lissa jumped when something brushed against her. But it was only Lia's hand, reaching for Alissa's.

"You frightened me!" the princess exclaimed. Her words echoed in the narrow passage. Suddenly she was even more thankful that Lia was beside her.

"Oh, Alissa," whispered Lia. "This whole thing frightens me! Where are we going?"

Alissa didn't answer because she couldn't. She had no idea where they were headed. She'd never heard anyone talk about a hidden passageway in the castle. What was its purpose? And where did it lead?

Alissa and Lia stared about curiously. Their candles cast weak shadows on the rough walls. They could see that great stone arches supported the ceiling. Each arch had a shape carved into its central keystone. But masses of cobwebs made the shapes hard to see.

Ahead of them, the girls heard the sound of small clawed feet. Other than that, the silence was total.

The passage turned and began to dip. "It seems like it's leading downhill," noted Lia.

"I think we're going underneath the great hall," said Alissa.

At that, Lia held Alissa's hand even more tightly.

As they walked on, the going grew more difficult. The passageway narrowed, and stones littered the uneven floor.

At last the passage leveled out. Here the ceiling became higher, the floor and walls smoother. But as they passed under an archway—

Both girls felt the change at once. The air around them, which had been comfortable, turned cold and clammy.

"Where is that draft coming from?" asked Lia.

"I don't think it's a draft," said Alissa slowly. "I think the ghost is here with us."

Lia almost dropped her candle. "Mercy! Alissa, please stop it. I'm already scared enough!"

"Well, it makes sense!" Alissa argued. "If the ghost led us here, he must be nearby. And I think he wants us to keep going."

Alissa began to move faster. But in the dim light, she stepped on a stone and lost her balance. Her candlestick fell to the floor, and the flame went out.

"Drat! There goes my candle!" she cried. "Hold yours higher so I can see, Lia. I've got to find it."

She bent down and searched the floor. "There it is!" she finally exclaimed. "Against the wall."

Alissa grabbed her candle and started to her feet. But halfway up, she paused and stared at the wall.

"This is odd," she said thoughtfully.

"What?" asked Lia. She knelt beside Alissa.

"It looks like there's a crack in this wall," Alissa said. "I wonder..."

Alissa placed the flat of her hand near the long crack. She pressed gently. Nothing happened.

She pressed harder. Slowly a door-sized piece of wall swung back.

"It's another passage!" Alissa cried. "And it opens up the same way as the first!"

Both girls peered through the opening. "Well, let's see where this goes," Alissa said.

"I'm not sure we should," began Lia. But it was too late. Her friend had already disappeared through the opening. Lia followed slowly.

This time, instead of another passage, they found a small square room. It was empty and bare, except for a door in the middle of one wall.

Alissa lit her candle from Lia's. Then she hurried to the door and lifted the iron bar that held it closed.

She took a step forward. "It's a cell!" she exclaimed. "Now why would this be here? There's already a dungeon at the back of the castle."

The girls entered the tiny cell. A simple bed stretched along one wall. The only other furniture was a rough table. A wooden bowl and a thick candle sat on top of that.

Alissa began studying the stone walls. "What are you doing?" asked Lia.

"Looking for clues," replied Alissa. "Maybe whoever was held prisoner here wrote something on the walls. It's so hard to see, though. I need more light."

Lia stepped closer, but her candle didn't help.

"I know," said Alissa. "We'll use this too." She lit the fat candle that stood atop the table.

By the light of the three candles, the girls searched the walls for clues. But there was nothing to be found.

Alissa paused and sniffed. "What's that?" she asked. "It

smells like burning paper."

Her eyes went to the thick candle. It was burning oddly. Small flames hissed and shot from its surface.

"This isn't a real candle!" Alissa cried. She knocked it off the table. The strange candle hit the stone floor, and the flame went out.

Both girls stared at the smoky mess. Alissa poked at the still-warm object with one finger before picking it up. "It's definitely wax on the outside," she said. "But there's something else underneath."

"It looks like a bunch of papers," said Lia.

"You're right!" Alissa exclaimed. "They've been rolled up and then covered in wax. Someone must have been trying to hide them!"

Alissa freed the papers from their wax cocoon. "There's writing!" she cried, smoothing out the top sheet.

"What does it say?" asked Lia.

Alissa peered closely. "It's hard to tell," she said. "The ink is faded."

"And it looks like some of it got burned," added Lia.

"Some," Alissa agreed. "But there's still enough...Oh, Lia!" she gasped. "This is it! This is what the ghost wanted us to find!"

"Whatever do you mean?" asked Lia.

Alissa looked up, a happy smile on her face. "This was written by Sir Grendon!"

CHAPTER TEN

Grendon's Plea

Sir Grendon!" cried Lia.

"Yes! Listen!" said Alissa. She read the words written on the top page, "'To my young friend.'" Then she turned to the last page and pointed to the words at the bottom. "See, it's signed, 'Grendon, Steward of Arcadia'!"

"I don't understand," said Lia. "Did he hide this here before he left the kingdom?"

"And who's his 'young friend'?" asked Alissa. "Well, maybe Grendon himself will tell us. Let's start reading."

"But not here," suggested Lia. "Our candles will be used up before we can finish."

"You're right," said Alissa. She led the way back to the great hall. At the end of the secret passage, they stopped.

"I'll check to be sure no one is about," whispered Lia. She lifted the tapestry and peered out. "It's all clear," she reported.

Alissa and Lia slipped into the room.

"We have to close this door," said Alissa. "But I want to be sure we can open it again. Now where exactly did I push it?"

Alissa pressed her hand against the wall in several spots.

61

"I think this is it," she finally said. She blew out her candle, licked her fingers, and rubbed them against the wick. Then she pressed one finger against the stone. When she lifted her hand, a dirty fingerprint could be seen.

"Let's see if it works," Alissa said. She closed the passageway door. "Right here," she announced, pushing on the spot marked by her fingerprint. The opening appeared again.

"Perfect!" she said. The girls closed the door and checked that the tapestry hung in place. Then they stole upstairs to their chambers.

There they curled up on Alissa's bed and spread out the papers. For a long time, they read in silence. At last they finished. With a shake of her head, Alissa sat up.

"I knew it!" she exclaimed, rubbing her tired eyes with a fist. "Grendon wasn't a coward at all! He didn't desert Arcadia or the young king."

"It's so sad," said Lia. "The baron locked up poor old Grendon in that tiny cell. And all because of your great-grandfather's will." She reread the page in her hand:

> The king's will makes it all clear. In it he names me as regent to look after Arcadia and his young son.
>
> Baron Mendor longs to get his hands on that will. He knows it will strip him of all power. But I have hidden it away so he cannot destroy it.
>
> The baron promises to free me if I tell him where the will is hidden. However, I do not believe him. In any case, I would never betray my king.

"The will must be inside that small chest we saw in Grendon's portrait," said Alissa. "But where on earth did he hide it? The only clue we have is what he says here." She went on reading:

I will try to find a way to get these pages to you, my young friend. But I fear that my message may fall into the baron's hands. So I dare not tell you in plain words where the will is hidden.

I leave you with these clues: There is something for you in the usual spot. It is the key to the key that unlocks the hiding place of the king's will. Should you need more guidance, look to my portrait. I hope it will shed some light on my words.

I am sorry to leave you with this task. But my wife and son are away from the kingdom. I fear that I shall never see them again. My body is weak, and I feel my years.

Take care, little one.

"Well, you've done it, Alissa," said Lia. "By finding this journal, you've discovered the truth about Sir Grendon."

"You mean *we've* done it," Alissa told her. Then she sighed. "But I don't think we're finished yet, Lia. We have to find my great-grandfather's will."

"Why?" Lia asked. "What difference can it make after all this time?"

"We need the will to completely clear Grendon's name," Alissa said. "Don't forget what he wrote at the very end." She flipped to the last page and read aloud:

I shall not rest until the king's will is made known to the people of Arcadia.

"Don't you see?" said Alissa. "That's why Grendon's ghost is walking. He can't rest until we find the will! He wants the truth to be known. And I want justice to be done."

She put the page down and rested her chin on her hands. Finally she looked up. "I think it's time to get some help," she said. "But I don't want to cause any more problems. So I'll talk to the one person who won't get upset by questions."

"Balin!" cried Lia.

"That's right," said Alissa. She gathered up the papers. "Are you coming along?"

"Yes," replied Lia. "I want this settled as much as you do."

~

The sun was just rising when Alissa and Lia reached the wizard's tower.

"I haven't been here in a while," said Alissa. "And never this early. I hope he doesn't mind."

She rapped gently on the door.

"Begone!" squawked Bartok from the other side.

They heard Balin say, "Hush, Bartok. It's Alissa and Lia."

"How does he know who's here?" wondered Lia.

"I don't completely understand it. He just always does," answered Alissa.

The door swung open, and Balin stared down at them. "Well, princess, it's been some time since I've seen you," he said. "And even longer since Lia honored me with a visit."

"I know," replied Alissa. "But a great deal has been going on."

"Yes," said the wizard as he stepped back to invite them in. "I do have my ways of keeping up with news. And you have set the castle folk buzzing."

Alissa's reply came in a rush of words. "Oh, Balin! I know I've upset some people. But I didn't try to. And wait until you hear what we've found out!"

"Sit," said the wizard as he settled himself in a chair. "And tell me."

It took some time to share the tale. When Alissa and Lia

finished, Balin nodded. "So your spell worked, princess. Excellent. But even better is how much you both discovered by using wits instead of magic."

Thoughtfully he stroked his beard and studied the pages in his hand. "I've always felt there was more to the story of Grendon."

The wizard gave the journal back to Alissa. "Well, what do you plan to do next, ladies?"

"We need your help, Balin," said Alissa. "I'm sure Grendon never told the baron where the will was hidden. So it must still be around here. We think it's in the chest that appears in the portrait. We just don't know where to find the chest."

"The clues in Grendon's papers don't help much," Lia added. "The key Alissa found in her pitcher might be the thing he left for the young friend to find. But what did he mean by 'the key to the key'?"

"Balin, suppose you used your magic," suggested Alissa. "Can't you 'read' something from the journal and key? Find clues that we can't?"

"I doubt it," said Balin. "I can read the thoughts and feelings of living people from some objects. But even my crystal ball won't help me with someone so long dead. And I wasn't able to read anything from the journal pages, Alissa—except the words that Grendon actually wrote."

"Could you try the key?" Alissa begged. "Please?" She held it out to him.

When the wizard's fingers touched the key, he jerked back as if burned. Then he held out his hand again. He took the key and stared at it steadily. "Someone still alive has held this," he said softly.

"Well, of course," said Alissa impatiently. "I have. And so

has Lia."

"No," said Balin. "Someone else. Now please be quiet!"

He folded his fingers around the key and closed his eyes. For a long time, no one made a sound.

Then Balin's mouth curved in a smile. He murmured, "I never would have guessed. Such a quiet child. I didn't pay her much attention. Not at all like the other one, who was noisy, bossy, bright, stubborn. Much like..." He shook himself and opened his eyes. Alissa and Lia were staring at him in wonder.

"Forgive me," he said. "For a moment, I was lost in the past."

"But you *do* know who held the key!" guessed Alissa. "It was the young friend, wasn't it? And you know who that was!"

Balin handed the key back. "You need to talk to your great-aunt, princess."

"Talk to Matilda?" exclaimed Alissa. "I can't do that. She can't be Grendon's young friend. She just can't!"

"Not Matilda," said Balin. "The quiet one." He smiled. "Go and talk to Maude."

CHAPTER ELEVEN

Another Ghost?

M aude!" cried Alissa and Lia in one voice.

"You can't be serious, Balin," Alissa said. "Surely Great-aunt Maude isn't the one Grendon expected to find the king's will! She can hardly find her way to the dinner table!"

"Come now, Alissa," said Balin calmly. "There's much you don't know about Maude. Or about Matilda, for that matter."

Alissa shook her head. "I just don't see how Maude could help us solve this mystery."

"All the more reason to talk to the good lady," said Balin with a laugh. "And I suggest you get started now."

Alissa and Lia said good-bye and started down the tower stairs. As they made their way to the bottom, they talked about what they had learned.

"I still can't believe Maude was Grendon's young friend," Alissa said.

"Well, you did say that your great-aunts were children when Grendon was alive," said Lia. "And I thought of something else. Maude may be the only person who's never told you to stop asking questions about Sir Grendon."

"You're right," said Alissa. "And I forgot to ask her too."

"I think a lot of people forget about Maude," said Lia softly.

There was little time to rest that morning before meeting with the great-aunts. And during the lesson, the girls had a hard time paying attention. They kept thinking about how to speak to Maude—alone. But that seemed hopeless.

Lia did her best. At the end of the lesson, she said, "Lady Matilda, I'm having trouble with my embroidery. So I was wondering if you might come back to my room to help me."

Matilda was pleased. It was unusual for either girl to ask for extra lessons. "Why, Lia, I'd be happy to," she replied.

Matilda followed Lia to the door. Then she looked back at Alissa. The princess was standing near Maude.

"Alissa, dear, you come along too. Your embroidery skills are in more need of help than Lia's, after all."

Alissa darted a helpless look at Lia. "I thought I might keep Great-aunt Maude company while you're gone," she said.

"Maude has no need of company just now," sniffed Matilda. "She has quite enough to do."

Alissa glanced at Maude. As usual, her great-aunt's lap was a snarl of needlework. Alissa shook her head and followed Matilda. She didn't notice the look of interest that Maude gave her.

At last the embroidery lesson was over. Matilda left, satisfied that she had fixed Lia's work. Alissa's was another matter.

"I'm sorry," said Lia when the girls were alone. "I never thought she'd make you come too!"

"I guess *I* should have asked for the lesson," said Alissa. "She probably would have let you stay with Maude."

The princess dropped down onto a footstool. "What do we do now? The great-aunts are always together. And we don't dare mention Grendon if Matilda's nearby. She's already angry about this ghost business."

Lia agreed. "We don't want to make her even angrier."

"So we'll just have to hunt for the will ourselves," said Alissa. "Even if we don't completely understand the clues."

She yawned mightily. "Oh, Lia, all this ghost hunting is wearing me out. I think we should nap for a while. Tonight, when everyone is asleep, we'll explore the passage again. It still makes sense that the will is somewhere in there."

"I hope we find it," said Lia. "Then Grendon can rest."

Alissa gave a tired smile. "And so can we."

It was unusually quiet in the castle that afternoon. Both Alissa and Lia slept long and hard. If a serving maid hadn't called them to dinner, they might have slept even longer.

At dinner they once again sat between the two great-aunts. Halfway through the meal, Matilda turned and began speaking to the lady who sat at her other side.

"Lia, see if you can ask Maude about Grendon while Great-aunt Matilda isn't listening," whispered Alissa.

Lia turned. But Maude's head rested on her hands, and her eyes were closed.

Lia whispered, "Unless Lady Maude talks in her sleep, it looks like we'll have to wait."

~

That night Alissa and Lia made their way to the great hall. Thanks to Alissa's fingerprint, they had no trouble opening the secret passageway.

69

"Should I close the door behind us?" asked Lia.

"No. We might not be able to get out," Alissa answered. "Let's just be sure the tapestry hides the opening."

The girls set off. The dark passage didn't seem quite so frightening this time.

Soon they reached the cell where Grendon had spent his last days. The door stood open, just as they had left it.

Alissa paused for a moment and looked into the gloomy little room. "Don't worry, Sir Grendon," she said softly. "We'll find the will so you can rest at last."

She led the way past the cell and into new territory. The passage quickly became more twisted. In some spots, the walls were cracked. Pieces of rock had fallen to the floor.

"Do you think it's safe here?" Lia asked in a worried voice.

Alissa glanced up at the stone arches. "I don't know," she admitted. "There doesn't seem to be anything here anyway. So let's head back."

"Maybe we can get the clues we need from Lady Maude," Lia said.

The girls walked back past the cell. Suddenly Alissa stopped. "Wait!" she whispered.

"What is it?" Lia asked.

Then Lia felt it too. The air was cold and clammy—just as it had been the night before.

Alissa crept forward, but she saw nothing. Then she looked back the way they'd come.

"Lia!" she cried. "The ghost!"

In the passageway, a misty figure swayed in the candlelight.

"Glory be!" breathed Lia.

"Let's go!" cried Alissa.

The girls chased after the figure. But the ghost did its vanishing act once again.

Alissa leaned her head against an archway. "If he doesn't want to talk to us, why does he keep appearing?" she groaned.

"Shhh!" hissed Lia. "I hear something!"

Alissa held her breath. At first she heard nothing. But then it came—a soft rustling sound. And it was coming from the direction of the great hall.

"I don't think it can be Sir Grendon," she whispered. "His ghost has never made any noise before."

"You mean there's *another* ghost?" cried Lia in a panic.

"I don't know. But someone—or something—is here," replied Alissa.

Quickly she pulled her friend to the other side of the archway. The girls flattened themselves against the rough wall.

The faint sound came closer and closer.

CHAPTER TWELVE

The Young Friend Speaks

lissa and Lia blew out their candles. Even so, the passage wasn't completely dark.

Alissa peeked around the edge of the arch. She caught sight of a flickering light.

At once Alissa ducked back. But as she did so, her elbow hit the rough stone wall. She couldn't help herself. "Ohhh," she groaned.

In return, someone let out a scream. Alissa was about to turn and run the other way when she realized something. The voice sounded familiar.

Gathering up her courage, she stepped into the middle of the passage. A shadowy figure stood before her, a candlestick in one shaking hand. The figure's other hand was pressed against the wall for support.

"Great-aunt Maude!"

"Alissa," replied Maude in a faint voice. "You frightened me."

"*I* frightened *you!*" cried Alissa. "What are you doing here?"

Maude paused. Finally she said, "I was following you."

"Why?" asked Lia.

"Well, I—" began Maude.

But Alissa interrupted. "You knew we wanted to talk to

you!" she exclaimed.

Maude nodded. "I did wonder if that's what you were trying to do."

"We were," said Lia. "Because we know you're the young friend Sir Grendon wrote to."

But now Maude just looked at them blankly. Suddenly Alissa remembered that her great-aunt had never found the journal. She didn't know what Sir Grendon had written. And she probably had no idea what had really happened to the steward.

"We found a journal that Sir Grendon kept," she said. "We think he addressed it to you. It was in the secret cell where he was held prisoner."

"Prisoner!" Maude cried. She lifted her chin. "Show me," she said. "I need to see."

So the girls led Maude down the passageway. On the way, they explained about the journal and the will. And they told her what had happened to Grendon.

They reached the room where Grendon had spent his last days. Maude slowly looked around. "He never left us," she whispered. A tear made its way down one cheek. "I knew he hadn't. But no one would believe me."

"What of the king's will, Great-aunt?" Alissa asked. "What do you know about that?"

"Very little," Maude replied. "What I do know, I'll gladly tell you. But not here. It's too horribly sad here."

"Come back to my room," suggested Alissa.

"That's a good idea," Maude agreed. "I'd welcome the chance to sit down. I'm an old woman. A very tired one, too, after staying up to follow you."

Alissa led the way back to the great hall. Once the door

was closed and hidden by the tapestry, the three headed upstairs.

In Alissa's room, Maude sank into a chair. For a long time, she was quiet. When she finally began to speak, the words poured out.

"For many years, I had the clues Grendon talks of," she began. "But until tonight, I had no idea what they meant. The king's missing will! If only I had been more clever."

Maude sighed. "But I'm not, so I found a clever person to solve the mystery for me. You, Alissa."

Alissa stared at her great-aunt. "You mean..."

Maude nodded. "Yes, I was the one who hung the portrait in the gallery. And the one who removed it. I also put the key in your water pitcher."

"That was you then. Not the ghost?" Alissa asked.

"Yes, it was me. I heard you talking about your history lessons with Sir Drear. And about the tour of the gallery he had planned for you. I thought it was the perfect time to bring out the portrait again. I was sure it would make you curious. And when it did, I left the key for you to find."

"But where did you get those things?" asked Lia.

"Ah, well, I should begin at the beginning," Maude said. "Matilda always complains that I get things mixed up."

She went on. "When I was a child, I spent a great deal of time with Sir Grendon. I'd sit in a corner of the accounts room. He'd work away at his books while I read. Sometimes he'd stop and tell me stories..." Her soft voice died away.

Alissa patted her great-aunt's hand. "You still miss him, don't you?" she said.

"Yes," whispered Maude. "He was a good, gentle man. And he knew how lonely I was. Even then, Matilda had little time for me."

Maude shook her head as though to clear her memories. "But the plague came. The queen fell ill. And next the king. Then one day, Grendon was gone. Everyone said he'd run away. But I knew that couldn't be true.

"One night I stole into the accounts room. I wanted to look in a hiding place that only we two used. A secret drawer in his desk. Grendon sometimes hid treats there for me to find. I thought he might have left a message."

"And did he?" asked Lia.

"Of a sort," replied Maude. "I found the key there. And a note. I think he must have written it at the last minute. Just as the baron's men came for him. All it said was 'my portrait.'"

She continued. "I knew the key must be to something important. I just couldn't figure out what that might be."

"So what did you do?" asked Lia.

"I went to look for the portrait. But it had been taken away. Perhaps by the baron. Or by Thaddeus, Grendon's son. Thaddeus returned to Arcadia after his father disappeared. Just like Drear, he was ashamed of Grendon."

"But you did find the portrait," Lia said.

"Yes. I kept looking and looking. After many months, I found it in a dusty old storeroom. As Grendon had told me to do, I studied the portrait for clues. I decided that the key must unlock the door or the chest."

"That's what we thought too," said Alissa.

"I recognized the tapestry in the portrait as one from the great hall. And I remembered an old door there. Only the king and steward used it."

"So there *was* a door!" exclaimed Lia.

"Yes," replied Maude. "But when I went to look for it, it

was gone. I almost never went into the great hall in those days. So I didn't know when the door had disappeared. I asked some servants what had happened. One told me that Baron Mendor had ordered the door to be walled over. The baron said the passage behind it wasn't safe."

BARON MENDOR

Alissa slowly nodded. "The baron must have decided to lock Grendon up in the passageway. And had the secret opening made where the door had been."

Maude looked at Alissa curiously. "How did you ever find the opening?"

"Lia recognized the tapestry from the portrait," Alissa explained. "That night we searched behind it. And when I pushed on the wall, it opened!"

Lia thought of another question. "How did you hide the portrait all these years, Lady Maude? And where is it now?"

"It's where it's always been. In plain sight, right in my room. I tacked some of my embroidery to the back of it and hung it with that side out."

She smiled. "Matilda has always hated my messy needle-work. Especially that piece. She's never really taken a close look at it."

Alissa and Lia laughed. There was more to Maude than they'd realized.

For several moments, all three were silent. Then Lia said, "All right. This is what we know: Grendon hid the king's will. He left the key and his portrait as clues to the secret passage. But we still have to find the chest—and the will. Unless we do, we can't fully clear Grendon's name. So we have to figure out just what he meant by his words 'the key to the key.'"

Alissa broke in. "I'm sure that the chest must be in the passage somewhere. With the will inside."

She looked at Maude. "You said only the king and steward used that door. Maybe they had a secret hiding place there— just like you and Grendon did in the accounts room."

"We've searched the passage already," objected Lia. "If there's a secret hiding place, I don't know where it is."

But Alissa had been thinking. "There is one more clue," she said. "And I think it will show us exactly where to look!"

The Key to the Key

hat clue?" Lia and Maude asked at the same time.

"The cold, clammy air in the passage," said Alissa. "Both times we felt it in the same place."

"You're right," said Lia thoughtfully. "And that's where we saw the ghost."

"I think he was telling us where to look," said Alissa. "I wish we could go back and explore that spot now. But there isn't time. We'll just have to do it late tomorrow."

"Which means another long night," sighed Lia.

Alissa turned to Maude. "Do you want to come with us again?"

"Thank you, dear, but no," said Maude. "This is work for those far younger than I am. I'll leave the matter in your hands."

Maude got to her feet. "Now I'm going to crawl into my bed before Matilda discovers I'm missing. All this talking has made me uncommonly tired." She kissed both Alissa and Lia. Five minutes later, all three were asleep.

By nightfall Alissa and Lia were again ready to search for the will. They stole downstairs, through the great hall, and back into the dark passageway.

Alissa led the way to a point between the entrance and Grendon's cell. "I'm sure this is where we felt the change in the air," she said. "And where the ghost appeared to us last night."

The girls placed their candlesticks on the floor. Then they began to go over the stone walls inch by inch. They pressed and pushed, looking for a secret hiding place. But they found nothing.

Finally Alissa sank down to the cold floor. Before long Lia joined her there.

"'The key to the key,'" Alissa said, repeating the words Grendon had written in his journal. "Great-aunt Maude thought I'd be clever enough to figure it out. But I'm not." She leaned her head against the wall.

"Maybe we're missing something," suggested Lia. "We haven't checked the top part of the wall, where we can't reach."

"I know," agreed Alissa. "I suppose it might be there." Her eyes moved along the upper row of stones and came to a stop. She stared at the center stone of the arch closest to them. "Why do you suppose there's a crown carved into the arch?" she asked.

"I don't know," said Lia. She pointed to another archway. "Each arch is different. That one has a throne."

"Do you suppose the carvings mean anything?" asked Alissa as she scrambled to her feet. She walked along, checking overhead. "Here's a flag," she noted.

Lia studied the arches. "Not many people have ever used this passageway. So it does seem strange that the keystones would be decorated."

Alissa stopped in her tracks. "Lia! That's it!"

"It is?" said Lia. "What is?"

"What you just said—'keystones'!" answered Alissa.

"Well, that *is* what you call the middle stone of an arch," said Lia. Suddenly her jaw dropped and she stared at Alissa. "Oh, Alissa! Grendon's words: 'The key to the key.' Do you suppose—"

"I do!" Alissa replied. "Let's check the other side of the archway closest to where the ghost appeared!"

And there it was—the last clue. On the center stone was carved the outline of a key.

"Quick!" said Alissa. "We have to find a way to get up there!"

"The table!" cried Lia. "If you stand on that, you'll be able to reach."

The girls ran into Grendon's cell. They dragged out the table and placed it under the arch. Alissa held on to Lia for support and climbed up.

Alissa reached out and gently traced the outline of the key with her fingertips. "Please," she whispered. Then she pushed.

Slowly the keystone moved. It opened up to show—

"The secret hiding place!" breathed Lia.

CHAPTER FOURTEEN

Justice Is Done

s anything in there?" Lia asked in excitement.

"I can't see," replied Alissa. "But..." She stuck her hand into the space behind the stone. Her fingers touched something cold and hard.

"I think it's the chest," she called down. Hardly daring to breathe, Alissa pulled out a small golden box.

Lia helped her friend climb down. Then both girls studied the chest. It looked just like the one in Grendon's portrait! There was even the same golden lock surrounded by glowing emeralds and rubies.

Alissa removed the key that hung around her neck. Without speaking, she stuck it into the keyhole. The lock clicked open!

"We found it!" cried Alissa after lifting the lid. "We found my great-grandfather's will!" She held up a rolled document. It bore the seal of the king, still unbroken. And on the outside of the roll were the words, "Final Will of King Garrick of Arcadia."

"I can't wait to read it," said Lia.

Alissa looked at the document. "Neither can I. But we can't—not yet."

"Why?" asked Lia.

"It wouldn't be right," said Alissa. "Only my father should break the seal."

"I hadn't thought about that," replied Lia. "Well, we should at least let Lady Maude know we found it."

"In the morning," said Alissa. "For now let's get some sleep." She placed the will in the chest but didn't lock the lid.

Before she left, there was one thing Alissa had to do. She walked down the passage to the cell where Grendon had spent his final days.

"You can rest now, Sir Grendon," she whispered. "Soon your name will be cleared. And the king's will shall be read at last." She softly closed the cell door behind her.

～

Much later the girls reported for their morning deportment lesson. Maude looked up as they came in, and Alissa winked at her. Quickly Maude ducked her head to hide her smile from Matilda.

The day's lesson tried Matilda's patience even more than usual. Alissa yawned every time she opened her mouth to answer a question. Lia's mind seemed to be somewhere else completely. But the last straw was when Maude started to giggle for no reason at all.

"I think that's enough for today," announced Matilda with a cross look. As the girls left the room, they heard her hiss at her sister. "Really, Maude! I wish I could count on you to set a good example." Alissa and Lia covered their mouths to silence their own laughter.

Back in Alissa's chambers, they didn't have long to wait for

Maude.

"Well?" Maude said as she took a seat. "Did you find it?"

Alissa reached under her bed and pulled out the chest. She carried it to Maude and placed it in her great-aunt's lap.

"Here it is," she stated. "The king's will—just as Grendon said."

Maude's hands shook as she opened the chest. She stared at the will but didn't touch it. Then she raised shining eyes to Alissa. "I knew you could do it," she said.

"Not without your help," replied Alissa. She turned to Lia. "I'm so excited! I can't wait for Father to see this. He won't believe it! And the look on Drear's face will be a sight to behold."

Lia poked her friend and pointed to Maude. Alissa's great-aunt was again staring at the will. She hadn't said another word.

In that moment, Alissa realized how much this discovery meant to Maude. And she knew what she wanted to do.

"Tomorrow is the Court of Justice," Alissa said to her great-aunt. "I think you should present the will to the king then."

Startled, Maude raised her eyes to Alissa. "I could never do that, Alissa. Not in front of everyone."

"But you're the one who has believed in Grendon all these years," said Lia.

"And the one who got us started searching," added Alissa. "So you should be the one to clear Grendon's name."

"I just can't, Alissa. You do it, please." Maude's eyes begged Alissa to agree.

"All right," said Alissa slowly. "It will be an honor."

For the rest of the day, Alissa and Lia talked about what Alissa should say. By the next morning, the princess felt as ready as she'd ever be. She waited just outside the great hall for the Court of Justice to begin.

Trumpets sounded. King Edmund entered the crowded hall and walked to his throne. Sir Drear already stood nearby. His eyes darted back and forth as he watched over the chest at his feet. The box was filled with gold and jewels.

The trumpets sounded again. This time Alissa moved through the hall to take her place at her father's side. Lia, as her lady-in-waiting, stood beside her.

For the next few hours, the people of Arcadia came before their king. A dishonest peasant was charged with stealing from a neighbor. The king listened to the man's excuses. Then he sentenced him to a day's work in the castle bakery. The bread he baked was to go to his neighbor.

A shepherd who had saved three of the king's sheep was thanked. Then the king gave the man a gold coin from the treasure chest.

Alissa sat and watched with pride. Her father treated everyone kindly and fairly. She could understand why the people of Arcadia loved him so.

Finally the last case had been heard. People stirred and began to head for the doors.

It was time. Alissa stood and called out, "Your majesty, may I present another case?"

A look of shock came over Sir Drear's pinched face. The steward began to sputter under his breath, "This is unheard of. All cases are to be announced beforehand, sire."

But the king simply nodded to Alissa. "We are listening, princess."

Alissa spoke in a clear voice. "King Edmund, I bring before you a very old case. One of terrible injustice. And I beg

of you to set things right."

She continued, "Long ago Arcadia had a good and honest steward. His name was Sir Grendon."

Sir Drear turned pale. King Edmund frowned. But he looked at Alissa's serious face and motioned her to go on.

"It has been said that Sir Grendon deserted his king and his country. But I can prove that this was not so."

Alissa turned to her lady-in-waiting. Lia took the chest, the key, and the journal from a bag. She handed them to Alissa. And Alissa in turn gave them to her father.

"What is all this?" asked King Edmund. First he looked through the pages of the journal, reading quickly. "This is written by Sir Grendon himself," he said.

Then he used the key to unlock the chest. He pulled out the rolled document and studied the seal. "My grandfather's will!" he exclaimed.

For a moment, King Edmund just stared at his daughter. Then he broke the seal and unrolled the old document. He read it to himself before rising to speak to the crowd. "The princess is right," he announced.

He turned to Drear. "Your grandfather has been greatly wronged, Drear. Sir Grendon never left Arcadia. He was held prisoner by Baron Mendor. He died protecting the hiding place of the king's will. A will that named Grendon—not the baron—as regent."

The king sat down again and motioned to his daughter. "Please go on, Alissa. Tell us where you found these things."

Alissa began her story. Everyone was silent as she spoke. The only exception was a gasp from Matilda as Alissa spoke of Maude's role. At the sound, Maude smiled and calmly met her sister's stare.

When Alissa finished, the king took a deep breath. "Thank you, princess. We now know the truth about Sir Grendon. The only thing left to decide is how justice should be served. You are the one who brought this matter before me, Alissa. Perhaps you have some ideas."

Alissa hadn't expected this. She thought for a moment. Then she raised her head and looked into her father's eyes. "I do have some ideas. I think your majesty should send word to every city in Arcadia. That way everyone in the kingdom will know of Sir Grendon's bravery. And his portrait should be hung in the gallery in a place of honor."

The king looked toward his steward. "Is that acceptable to you, Sir Drear?" he asked.

For once Drear was at a loss for words. "I...I...I...Yes, sire. It would bring great honor to my grandfather."

"Very well," King Edmund announced. "So be it. And the thanks of all of Arcadia to you, ladies." He nodded to Maude, Lia, and Alissa in turn.

Then the king brought the Court of Justice to a close. As everyone began leaving, Sir Drear stepped forward. He bowed to Alissa. "Princess, I must say...I mean...What I'm trying to say..."

Alissa smiled. "I understand, Sir Drear. What you're trying to say is how proud you are of your grandfather. And what a wonderful steward he was."

"Yes, that's it," said Drear. He added in a low voice, "Thank you for giving him back to me."

Then Drear pulled himself together. In his usual voice, he said, "Of course, I should have paid closer attention to his portrait. After all, most of the gallery portraits give clues to some mystery about their subjects."

"What?" said Alissa in surprise. This was news to her.

"Oh yes, princess," said Drear. "That was the custom, you see. To have a portrait done in such a manner that it gave clues about one. Just as my grandfather's did about the hiding place he and the king often used. Well, good day, princess."

Alissa shook her head in wonder. Why hadn't Drear told them of this custom when they were in the gallery? Now she wanted to go back and look at all the portraits again. Just to see what kinds of clues she could pick up about the people in them.

She smiled to herself. Balin had been right after all. Drear *had* taught her something interesting. And she'd learned that history wasn't as dry and dusty as she'd thought.

However, the gallery would have to wait. Alissa had a few things to take care of first. The princess picked up Sir Grendon's journal and looked through it one last time. How she wished she'd known the man who wrote these words.

But when Alissa reached the last page of the journal, she stared in surprise. What had happened?

Alissa tucked the journal under her arm. She found Lia and whispered to her, "Come on. I've got to talk to Balin right away."

"About what?" asked Lia as she hurried along beside the princess.

"The journal!" said Alissa. "I just looked at the last page. And Grendon's final words are gone! I think Balin used his magic after all. And I want to know why!"

The girls made their way to the wizard's tower. At the top of the steps, Alissa hammered on the door. Without waiting for an answer, she opened the door and went in. Lia followed the princess into the room.

Balin looked up from his crystal ball. "Congratulations,"

he said.

"Oh, Balin," laughed Alissa. "I might have known you'd watch what happened in the crystal ball. I wanted to tell you all about it."

"I think you had another reason for coming anyway," said Balin.

"Yes," said Alissa. She put Grendon's journal on the table. "Just look what your magic has done," she said, pointing to the last page.

Balin moved closer. "I don't see a thing," said the wizard.

"That's the point," Alissa said. "This is where Grendon had written, 'I shall not rest until the king's will is made known to the people of Arcadia.' And now those words have disappeared!"

Balin sat back. "I had nothing to do with that," he calmly stated.

"You didn't?" said Alissa.

Balin shook his head. "No. As your father said, the thanks go to you and Lia and Maude. You are the ones who made the words vanish. For when the will was found, justice was done. And Grendon could rest at last."

He gently placed the journal in her hands. Slowly and silently, Alissa and Lia left the room.

As Alissa started down the stairs, she paged through the journal once again. The document had served its purpose. She really should turn it over to her father. Or Sir Drear.

But no, she decided. The journal should go where Grendon had meant it to go. She would place it in the hands of its rightful owner—Maude.